IMBROGLIO: THE MORNING OF THE MOGUL (BOOK 9)

PART III : DOLCE VITA

HICHEM KAROUI

GLOBAL EAST-WEST (LONDON)

CONTENTS

EPIGRAPH

"Nobody did a secret deal
Nobody was for sale
Nobody bent the rules at all
And nobody went to jail
And all of them were honest men
As white as driven snow
And lived on a higher plane
And shat on those below..."
Roger Woddis: All Clear

"And so, what could my sterile and uncouth genius beget but the tale of a dry, shrivelled, whimsical offspring, full of old fancies such as never entered another's brain — just what might be begotten in prison, where every discomfort is lodged and every dismal noise has its dwelling?"

Cervantes: Don Quixote (Prologue)

IMBROGLIO

The Morning of the Mogul
A wise report to a wise minister by a wise citizen
(A serialised novel)

Part III: Dolce Vita

Book 9: Imbroglio

Volumes in this series published by Global East-West (London)

Dedication

To the memory of Nana ...
Beloved mother...
You are always in my heart.
May you rest in eternal peace.

NOTES

NOTE OF THE PUBLISHER

This is Mister Bassam Bourasin's admitted report as a citizen of His republic. He didn't give it a name. He initially addressed it to the Interior Ministry. Instead, it landed on my desk. I publish it as is, with no major changes to its form or content. However, because the report is around 800 pages long, it was serialised and divided into three parts. The two previous parts have already been published.

Here is book Nine, starting Part III: *Dolce Vita.* Other volumes will soon follow in this last part of the series.

I also have to notice that this is a translation. The first draft was written in Arabic. The author had no intention of publishing it. In any case, it is understandably unpublishable in the country… for the same reasons that silence any samizdat in the Arab world today, like yesterday!

Hichem Karoui

Note of the Author

All of the individuals in my story, as well as the country, are not made up. However, even if some characters claim to be more fictive or strange, crazier or more foolish than others, they are not required to justify their location. My country can be found throughout the Arab world. Whatever name people give it, you won't notice a difference if you pay attention.

Bassam Bourasin

ONE

The trip lasted only a short time. I spent a week in the village idling and loafing, something I had never done before. I didn't notice the passage of time. I received a call from Hassan when the electricity and phone were fixed. It was not an unpleasant call in my frazzled and mournful state then.

He tried to console me by asking how I was doing. Although the scenario was not ideal, I said I was okay. The perpetrators were kind since they did not slaughter the entire community, something they could do perfectly. Then he asked if I planned to stay in 'Ouja for a long time. I explained that I was merely settling some critical matters before leaving and would only take three or four days. He said he had reserved a room for me at the Sheraton and notified the Minister of everything. I thanked him and the Minister for graciously caring for my humble person.

I hung up the phone and pondered for a few moments. I did not expect the events to go so far and so fast. Then, rethinking the situation, I became aware that I was trapped in an intricate imbroglio I had unintentionally provoked. But I hadn't wholly lied and couldn't be blamed for other people's stubbornness. First, I was convinced that the State owed me at least $13.500 million. Then, as I wanted to show how much I was attached to the fatherland, I said, "Patriotism is too flattering to discard even if it would cost me two $200 million." But, then, I don't know what devil pushed me to add, "Patriotism is too flattering to discard even if it would cost me two $200 million!" The last sentence was pure bragging. I did not mean it. Hassan was not supposed to take it seriously.

But as soon as his ears caught it, the sentence stuck to his mind like glue, and he became obsessed with the idea that the state owed me $200 million. He kept repeating it and pushing me to confirm. He was confident that it was the correct sum the government owed me. As the Director of National Security, he is better placed to know the truth. Could I oppose him? No, of course, I couldn't. Nor could I deny I said it. I felt he would have me killed if I did. So, I refrained. I'm not unwilling to receive the funds, though.

On the contrary, I've been working hard for fair compensation. Hassan knows what he's doing, and I would not ask him for any explanation. He'd ignore it. Who would argue with him? After all, I am flattered if a high-ranking administration official is persuaded that my skills are worth far more than I previously estimated.

I needed to prepare for the big day because I wanted to be ready for the meeting with the

Minister. My return to the capital, which I intended to be noticeable this time, had to be successful. I couldn't feel loose and powerless or practically crushed as I had in the past. On the contrary, I somehow felt confident, perhaps even like a conqueror.

Nonetheless, my entrance into the capital was less well-received than I had hoped. I did not take offence at this minor failing, though, because I know the entire country is going through unique circumstances. Citizens would have undoubtedly welcomed the new mogul's arrival in times of peace. But, oh! I don't expect them to queue on the sidewalks to receive me like they used to do for the King, the President, and their most important guests. Still, they would have spotted my blue car, the intrepid Zerga, rumbling and horning merrily on the road.

In reality, the streets were less crowded than they used to be. Moreover, it wasn't night-time when I arrived but early afternoon. The shops and stores were open, and people were lazily sprawling on café terraces in the central plaza and in front of the cinema gates. Without the apparent presence of the armed troops at crossroads and crossings and in front of official buildings, one may mistake it for a typical metropolis. Of course, that was not the case, but people were apathetic. There was an overall sense of indifference as if the nation had already surrendered to the will of the new masters. That was odd, considering that everyone knew about the civil war continuing outside the capital.

What was going on beneath their noses was unimportant to them! After all, it isn't exactly new. They got so used to coups and counter-coups that it doesn't matter whether they are ruled by a king, a president, an emir, or even a baboon, as long as they can live in peace! Unfortunately, however, peace is still out of reach. But who knows? In any case, they are far and away the last to be asked about their opinion. Even if some are foolish enough to believe that their opinion still matters! But will they dare to express it and risk passing into posterity as martyrs and heroes? I know from personal experience that many of those martyrs and heroes are dozing off behind jail bars. However, with chaos erupting in the country occasionally, it is difficult to determine who is the martyr and who is the hero!

Indeed, the heroes of one dictatorship are the unlucky cowards and traitors of another! During the King's reign, I was a coward, fearing Hamda La'war's retaliation and thus doing more to protect myself than because I was convinced of their nonsense. And even though I was the victim of a ruthless plot during the scoundrel's reign, I continued to play the game. That is why I am casually becoming the hero of the current dictatorship. I'm about to be decorated, whereas my former Parti's boss, one-eyed Hamda, is humiliated and hunted by the police, the militia, half the army, and a hoard of other jihadis who want to behead him publicly. However, I hope this is the last, most stable, permanent system. I want to think so if I don't want to be hunted down like the unfortunate one-eyed former Parti's boss by the next putschists anxious to rid the country of traitors and other bloody arrivistes.

Like most natives in this country, I had never been allowed to freely and consciously choose the Party, the government, or the men worthy of my trust. The authorities don't care about our trust; it is not accepted as a decent currency in the stock exchange, and they may be correct if they don't need it to manage the country and accumulate deposits at offshore banks. I was born during the War of Independence and grew up under the King's rule. When I started working at the bank, I was assigned to the formidable chief of the Party's cell. He brought me to his office one day and told me flatly, "You're required to work for us, Bassam."

I replied shyly, "It is a great honour for me, Mister Hamda, but I am already working for the bank." But, of course, I was young and naive then.

I spotted the one-eyed potentate's decaying teeth coloured by the stale tobacco he was smoking and his shiny face grinning atrociously like a mask. He eventually recovered, coughed slightly, and added, "You little joker, Bassam. I've known you since you were a child, running barefoot through the backstreets of 'Ouja, and I know your father well. He's a nice guy, though a little... well... simple-minded, right? Otherwise, he would have been a welcome addition to the Party."

"Yes, sir, he is not very complicated."

I resisted responding to his implication, which was a low-level provocation, because, as far as I recall, I had never gone barefoot in the backstreets. My father was an elderly man who, unbeknownst to me, was nearing the end of his life. So I wasn't looking for a fight with the mighty Hamda. If he said I was barefoot, ragged, or starving, or that my father is a simpleton, or anything else, I had to admit it and be grateful that he even condescended to receive me in his office, which was the first official office I had ever entered; apart from the bank, which at the time, I did not know was state-owned. Mister Hamda represented the Party. The Party was the government, and the government was the King. Who was I to oppose or argue with him? A man who was recognised almost as a saint. For whatever he touched was blessed by the State. I was a mere bank clerk rookie starting a career, thanks to the blessing of the Party's boss. I had neither the means nor the energy to confront the cyclone's translucent and authoritative single eye, which incorporated the Party, the motherland, and the State.

As a result, when Hamda stated, "I need you to be my eye, son," I didn't dare to giggle. Nor did I ask him, 'Which one, sir?' even though the thought crossed my mind. Instead, I said, "Yes, Mister Hamda, I will be your eye."

God knows it wasn't easy for me, but I couldn't act any other way because Hamda had methodically prepared his speech. And, before we got there, he lectured me on the virtues of the Party and the advantages its good militants obtained, emphasising that one cannot be a true patriot unless one joins the ranks of the Party, which is our only hope of retaining our independence; and barely covering his threatening hints and allusions to my job at the bank as being entirely dependent on my attitude towards him and his Party.

It was easy for him to persuade me. I didn't want to lose the job I had worked so hard for, and I knew he could harm me if I refused to cooperate. So even though the idea of writing secret reports about my coworkers and fellow residents seemed odiously nasty and immoral, I entrenched the little satrap's authoritative discourse and behaved. If I had any scruples, I would hasten to defend my actions by the undeniable debt that every citizen of this country owes to the national Party that protects us from foreign greed rather than by my own weakness and helplessness. Anyway, because spying for the Party was regarded as a patriotic act that elevated me to the status of a national hero, like Hamda - I didn't know his full tale then - I became enthusiastic, if not passionate. Hamda La'war is most likely in the south with the Scoundrel, while I am in the capital, where I was treated like a gentleman. I'm sitting in my magnificent room on the sixth story of the Sheraton.

***

When I parked my car in the hotel's large parking lot, a porter appeared and carried my suitcase with a big smile on his swarthy face. I went with him to the lobby. The middle-aged man behind the reception desk asked if I had made a reservation. At this hotel, I saw that everyone was happy.

"My name is Bassam Bourasin. Do you mind checking whether you already have my name on file?

The man flipped through his registers before

raising his head and saying, "Yes, sir; you're welcome. It is a great pleasure to have you in our hotel, sir. Would you please sign the visitor's book?"

I filled out the documents and signed them.

"Your luggage will be carried upstairs by the page. Your room number is 356. I wish you a pleasant stay with us, sir."

I thanked him and proceeded to the lift with the porter.

He opened the gate to my room, and I entered. He set the suitcase on a low carriage and drew the curtains. The light streamed into the tawny-walled room, revealing a lovely space to my eyes. The bed's sheets and blankets were flawlessly stretched, while the walls were adorned with modern art pictures. A large yellow carpet covered the floor, and the entire space exuded a salubrious neatness and a soothing silence.

I thanked the porter and gave him a tip. When he left, I went into the restroom. I'm still constantly overcome with diuretic urgency whenever I land in a new place! It may be the effect of climate change on my metabolism. I recall that the first thing I did as a new employee at 'Ouja Bank was to find the bathroom, and when I moved to my new flat, I had to unload my bladder as well. My first night in prison was also quite diuretic. I recollect earlier sojourns in several hotels of the capital, and strangely, the same reaction occurred everywhere; so, I assume that the activity of my bladder is mysteriously tied to my space tripping.

The bathroom's glowing state captivated me. I'll say it again: luminous! Everything within is bright, dazzling, beautiful, and almost embalmed. Even my face was mirrored on the glossy surface of the bathtub. It's wonderful! So wonderful! If I didn't know that the servants would gossip and make a fool of me, I would even live in the bathroom, eat and drink, write, and sleep in the bathroom. But taking me for an oddball would not improve my public image; it's the last thing I want. So, for the time being, I must focus on the following little details: I am no longer an unknown bank clerk working in a blackhole village that no one has heard of, but rather a VIP of the new dictatorship, and even my village is now famous as a result of the massacre. Besides, if I believe the Director of Security, whom I have no reason to doubt. I am wealthy, wealthy enough to purchase the Sheraton and other big hotels as well.

However, I must admit - at least to myself - that when I was not as wealthy as I am now (I can't say I was destitute either), it never occurred to me to eat or sleep in a hotel bathroom. It would have shocked me just thinking about it. But now, precisely because I've become wealthy, I have strange and crazy thoughts! Am I becoming an eccentric rich man? These are most likely the infallible signs of affluence. Many millionaires are known to be vagabonds and weirdoes. So, I'm presumably suffering from their weird symptoms.

But I must restrain myself. I'm only getting started in my new millionaire career, and if I start it off with these wild antics, what will I not do in a month or a year?

***

To begin, I resolved to act as if nothing had changed in my life. I would get up at the same time every morning and have the same breakfast, primarily of eggs, milk, and coffee. I'd then head to my office. I'd take a lunch break at one p.m. and then return to the office. I'd pick a little restaurant where I wouldn't be spotted. I may have my lunches in the Sheraton's restaurant here, but I know it is pricey. The bill would be exorbitant. And, while I am not required to pay for anything, I do not wish to appear greedy because I am Hassan's - or, more appropriately, the State's - guest. Anyway, I've never been a glutton, and my long career at the bank taught me to be cautious with money, for unscrupulousness leads men nowhere but to their own demise.

As for the dress, I would keep it in my personal closet. My clothing is modest but functional, although I may need a different status. A businessman, as I am expected to be, should be well-dressed. I would undoubtedly encounter prominent people, and I remember what Hassan mentioned about their attire. That's why he purchased me the sophisticated outfit I'm still wearing. I cannot afford to travel to Paris, Rome, or London only to go shopping like the Minister, Mr Mamduh - at least not right now, because they have yet to pay their loan or at least a portion of it. I'm confident that Hassan will assist me in obtaining a respectable little sum as a pre-payment on the account, allowing me to live decently.

Meanwhile, since I am in the capital, I should contact my bank's headquarters, although I doubt they will refund me for the five months I spent in jail. I did not notify them of my unexpected absence, nor did Mr Aroussi. How would I do it? The two guys who knocked on my door convinced me I was on an official trip over a government invitation. Could I disobey? Moreover, I found my boss out there, preceding me. Then, whom was I supposed to notify of my absence?

At the headquarter, they are probably aware that Mr Aroussi is in jail; they could not be unaware of his detention because he was on his way to a meeting with the Chairman when he was arrested. As for me, I needed to be more important in the bank's structure. Who cares about a clerk? I've been ignored, ditched. I am confident that the Chairman is unaware of my wealth; he would not have forsaken me if he had been. I've never met him in person, but I did catch a glimpse of his plump pinkish face during a conference. Even then, I had no idea that the big tall man giving a short welcoming address in the Hilton's spacious reunions room was the Chairman of our bank. My over-excited bladder had precisely chosen that moment to summon me to the loo. What a calamity!

When I returned, the Chairman had already concluded his speech and left the room. Mr Aroussi and other high-ranking bank officers walked him to the hotel door. I mistook him for the Minister of Finance, but I was updated by a colleague. I felt ashamed of my clumsy attitude, but I doubt the Chairman noticed. Unfortunately, I know some envious colleagues may report it, if not directly to the Chairman, then to one of his subordinates. That was embarrassing. I tried, all the same, to stay in my chair for the remainder of the session, although the speakers bored me to death.

I didn't yawn or exhibit any signs of tiredness. Instead, when it was Mr Aroussi's turn to speak, the volcanic activity of my rebel bladder became so irresistibly pressing that I would have urinated in my trousers if I didn't literally rush forward, crossing the room like an arrow to reach the lavatory far off in the corridor before the flood.

***

My irrelevant behaviour did not go undetected by the lecturer at that time. To my dismay, Mr Aroussi lifted his head just as I was leaving the room, and it seems to me that he even halted and scowled at me while I had my hand on the doorknob. I scurried away, overcome by crushing guilt, and hurried towards the toilet.

Odd! When I got there, the bloody mechanism broke down! My bladder was entirely jammed because I was so choked by my guilt. I stood, legs apart, in front of the urinal for a long time, waiting for the stream, but nothing happened.

Meanwhile, as I struggled against my pain, a man entered the washroom, stood by my side, and relieved himself. Because he was much taller than me, I had the unpleasant sense that he was staring at me with blatant interest. On his way back to the door, he stood briefly in front of the glass to adjust his tie, but he remained looking at me sideways, increasing my nervousness. I flushed but didn't turn my head. I was sure he was asking himself some suggestive questions about the significance of my prolonged stay in the lavatory in that strange position if I wasn't doing what everyone else does in that situation. He even whistled an enigmatic melody from an old song while wagging his head and titillating in front of the glass. He was evidently pleased to see his face or purporting to communicate his cheerful mood while I was inwardly raging against my bladder. Finally, he condescended to leave, and only then did I irrigate the urinal.

Mr Aroussi was still speaking when I returned to the conference room. He locked his eyes on me so intensely that I thought he intended to pulverise me. So, with my tail between my legs, I sat awkwardly on my chair, no longer daring to look at him. I was expecting retaliation, but nothing occurred. My boss immediately forgot about the incident, but its memory has stayed with me.

Yet, I am still trying to figure out where Hassan intends to place me. If it is not at the Central Bank, then at the Ministry, I told myself. I should outline the plan of my grand project, as he requested. He wasn't kidding. Far from it, Hassan is a man who should be regarded seriously for every word he says.

My empathy is growing firm and persuasive.

"Make way for John Law... I'm coming!" I'm tempted to shout. Hip Hip! Hurray!

***

TWO

I am fortunate. I immediately discovered what I was missing to begin working actively on my project. After a decent shower and a honeyed snooze that afternoon, I left the hotel and wandered along the street, leaving my car, Zerga, sunbathing in the park. I spotted a bookshop whose glass case caught my eye, for it was selling various Islamic books. I came to a halt and looked at the titles and names of the authors, and I noticed that many were not Arabs. They were from India, Pakistan, Iran, and other countries whose original language was not Arabic. But the books were translated versions. I went into the bookstore and asked the storekeeper, a plump and short Asian with a long white dishdasha, whether he had anything on banking. Many Asian citizens have lived in our country for many years and have earned the right to work but not the right to become citizens. The man I mistook for an Indonesian or a Malaysian turned out to be a Chinese from Sin-kiang, where most of the people are Muslims. He spoke Arabic fluently, albeit with an accent. As he returned with a book with the pompous title 'Islamic Banking' and placed it on the counter before me, I asked him why the books about Islam he was selling were not originally written in Arabic but translated from other languages.

– This is because the most important Islamist thinkers are not Arabs, sir, he said with a smile.

– The most important? I asked, a little shocked.

– Yes, sir, he confirmed.

The answer struck me. Whether this is true or not, I have no idea. I bought the book, spoke briefly with the Chinese, and promised to return in a few days.

About a half-hour later, as I was crossing the lobby of my hotel and walking towards the lift, I heard my name called. I turned, and I saw Suleiman Mughli approaching, all smiles, stretching his arms like Christ on an illusory cross, and shouting:

– My dear Bassam! It's great to see you here... and most of all, as a free man. Ha Ha Ha!

Suleiman wore a splendid grey suit with a white shirt and a blue tie, and his black shoes shone on the carpets. He was the last person I expected to see at this hotel. He walked a few steps and, grabbing me by my shoulders, held me in his arms as if I were a buddy he hadn't seen in years. Then he recommended we go to the hotel's cafeteria for a drink. I told him I was busy and would only be with him for five minutes.

– Even less, he said airily.

So we crossed the lobby oppositely and entered a long corridor with closed doors aligned on each side. We turned left and strolled into another gallery illuminated by white neons until we reached a spacious hall with pan-elled-glass walls and saw people sitting hither and thither on stools, chairs, and sofas, chatting and drinking, and nobody seemed to notice us.

We proceeded to the counter and ordered two black coffees. Mughli searched his pockets for cigarettes, but anticipating what he wanted, I offered him one from my packet.

– No, he responded dismissively, these are useless to me. American mixed tobacco is my favourite. But what the hell! I thought you weren't a smoker.

– I am now as addicted as you, Mr Suleiman. The times are changing. I owe you.

– You don't mean it.

– Of course, I mean it. The packet you handed me was only the beginning. I've been smoking every day since then.

– Ah! But the intention was good. I'm sorry

you didn't want more powerful stuff.

I ignored his drug allusion, but he wasn't waiting for an answer. He asked me:

– Did you see the others?

– What about the others? Who are you referring to?

– Your pals, lad. Your ex-colleagues.

I looked at him, bewildered, expecting some explanation, but he continued to smoke listlessly while sipping his coffee slowly. His eyes glittered and blinked as he turned his head towards the door. I followed his lead and looked at the door. To my amazement, I noticed three or four faces that were not wholly unfamiliar to me, and their appearance was so unexpected that I got disoriented for a moment, thinking I had returned to jail.

– Do you see them? Muttered the Mughli, pressing me.

Then it was true! I wasn't hallucinating. Mahmoud, the black guard, was leading Frankenstein, Zorro, and three other men, whom I assumed were all still in prison. They were strolling in a queue behind Mahmoud, hurrying towards an unknown destination. Because the cafeteria's translucent wall covered a large area, it was easy to see their movements from the counter.

– What exactly are they doing here? Where are they going?

– Never mind, he said; they're just doing their job.

– Working at the Sheraton?

– Yes, like you, at the library.

– This hotel is on the street, not in jail.

– The street? Mumbled the Mughli. It's not much different. Anyway, you should know that they send them on assignments to serve in hotels, hospitals, administrations, and so on any time they need help clearing out drains, washing dishes, fixing the roads, the pavement, the sidewalks, or anything else.

Then I remembered that some inmates used to go outside in the morning for specific tasks and return late in the afternoon. So the small group had vanished into the passageways without even noticing us.

– They are not after you, I wish! I turned to Mughli.

He laughed.

– Of course not. It's a coincidence, just like our meeting. (He paused for a time before adding,) Don't be afraid; I am free, just like you.

– I'm not afraid, Mr Mughli, I said. So, who are the others you were asking me about?

He lingered.

– I thought you saw them working in the garden, so I asked.

– Do you mean the same inmates?

He gave a nod.

– I was unaware of their presence at the Sheraton. In fact, I find it strange.

– You're right, he continued. Many strange things are happening now. I understand you are not from the capital, but you have the time to get a picture of the situation.

I'm not sure we were talking about the same things. To change the subject, I hastily added:

– I believe you have been released without trial. You have potent allies, Mr Suleiman.

He smiled at me and replied:

– As powerful as yours, Mr Bassam. We are both in the same case.

The comparison did not sit well with me. I was about to respond when he preceded me and asked:

– Aren't you waiting for Hassan?

– Yes, I do, said I.

– So do I.

– It's still early, he said, looking at his wristwatch. We have plenty of time; the business can wait.

– Business? Did I hear well? And with who else but the security director? It was exciting! But I didn't press him any more. He was probably lying, I reasoned, because I couldn't imagine the Director of Security flirting with a notorious member of the Mafia. What could they possibly talk about? What are their shared interests? Then I remembered that the Afghan, Hassan's rival, was trading guns with

Suleiman before his detention. What if Hassan learned about the Afghan's intention to depose him and sought a powerful ally? Without a doubt, Suleiman was uniquely qualified for the task. That could explain his unexpected release.

The Mafioso wasn't talkative, and I didn't annoy him with inappropriate questions. We finished our coffee and walked through the crowded cafeteria and corridors until we arrived at the lobby. We shook hands and parted ways as he suddenly recalled a critical meeting he had omitted.

I entered the lift and pushed the button for the sixth floor. Once in my room, I started to organise my affairs. The room was outfitted with a TV, a radio, a phone, a small fridge, a table with a virgin notebook, which I now use to write, two armchairs, and two sofas.

I opened my luggage and began hanging my clothing on the wardrobe hooks. I stuffed my documents into the drawer and covered them with my pants. It's a miracle that I could keep my private and ultra-secret notes away from hostile hands while in prison, and it's just normal that I keep them away from prying eyes today. I also need to keep the present notes safe. I considered slipping them beneath the mattress or under the carpet but instantly changed my mind. I'm done if a zealous housekeeper decides to chase the dust under the bed or the rug. However, unless he or she is a trained spy, they are unlikely to snoop under my underwear. But I have an advantage. Everyone in the hotel believes me above suspicion because the Director of Security or one of his employees booked this room for me, emphasising my importance to the government. So, who would dare rummage into my drawers?

***

THREE

Throughout the afternoon, I waited in vain for a call from Hassan. When it didn't happen, I assumed he was busy with the Mafioso, so I turned on the TV and relaxed on the bed in my shoes, watching an old film. I was tired and resolved not to take any unplanned steps. I couldn't leave the hotel for an extended period. When would Hassan decide to ring me? I have no idea and no mobile. I was just out of prison and almost out of touch with the new reality of the country to which I must adapt every day, every hour, every minute.

I started to feel a little hollow in my stomach around 8 p.m. Apart from a small sandwich,

I hadn't eaten anything. So I decided to get ready for dinner.

***

The blue evening was weaving its dark mantle about the balcony. I turned on the lights and dressed in a white shirt, a silky tie, and a dinner jacket. It was unnecessary to change my trousers, but I polished my shoes; and after one last look at the glass, I turned out the light and left the room.

When I was in the lift, a couple of Europeans walked in at the third landing; then, in a fraction of a second before the iron gate closed, it appeared to me that the two shadows slinking in the corridor, of whom I had caught a glimpse, are pretty identical to Hassan and the Mughli from the backside. I would have run after them, but the couple blocked the way. The gate closed before I could move; because the couple was smiling and saying good evening to everyone, I smiled back and nodded. The two other people were Arabs who were chattering loudly and bragging about Spanish castles. They were well-turbaned and clad in the traditional dishdasha that trailed to their ankles.

– Eight centuries we dwelled there, and for all that era, Spain was ours, said the younger, who appeared to be returning from a trip to Spain.

– Not just Spain said the elderly man. We should have stayed in France, Italy, Greece, and other Western nations. The Arabs were the world's rulers. Those castles you visited in Spain were spreading the light of knowledge and progress at a time when the entire European continent was still plunged into the darkest ignorance. The brightest minds in Europe are aware of their debt to Muslims, but they are resentful.

– They wouldn't be who they are if they weren't, the young guy retorted.

The European couple remained deaf and quiet. That dubious outburst of rage ashamed me. It was not generous. What happened to kindness and hospitality? Suppose the couple understands Arabic. What would they think of these two jerks?

– Dogs, they're all disbelieving dogs and sons of b*tches, the old man continued. Look at the epidemics they're spreading, alcohol, drugs, free sex, immorality. It is a complete break-down of values. Europe is a dog's dinner.

– When we lost the same values, we lost Spain, the young guy said.

– Look at these two...

But before the old man could add anything, we reached the ground, and the automatic gate opened. The two Europeans left, and I followed them across the lobby, which appeared more lively at that hour. A piece of sweat music was played on the piano. Several Arabs and foreigners were sitting on the sofas. The reception desk was crowded with arrivals, whose luggage was piled on the floor.

The pages were busy, and the movement was febrile. The small exchange agency remained open, as did the other shops and stores selling newspapers and magazines, tobacco, English and French pocket-books, stamps and post-cards, cameras, films, small batteries, sports clothes and utensils, bath costumes, and various souvenirs, handcrafted goods, watches, spectacles, traditional robes and turbans, daggers, copper plates, artificial palm trees and plastic camels, luxurious pipes, colourful rugs, silver ash-tray... It was just like the market at home. I lingered outside the window shops since I wasn't in a rush, hoping to see Hassan and the Maffiosi emerge, but it was in vain.

Finally, tired of the noise and dazzled by the lights, I pushed forward and turned to the left, walking along the bright corridor until I reached the restaurant where customers were already eating.

A stout young man in an immaculate white jacket, black trousers, and bow tie greeted me at the door and inquired, "Are you alone, sir?"

As I confirmed, the butler asked me to follow him, which I did. In the dark light of the candelabrums, the room was full of unfamiliar faces, busy eating and chatting. There were a few ladies. However, the majority of them appeared to be foreigners. The Arab women were appropriately muffled, disguised, and escorted by both children and husbands. The latter ate quietly or read the menu or a newspaper between courses to appear busy or important. They rarely address their wives and prefer to look elsewhere when not pretending to read.

***

I was seated at a table near the transparent glass wall. I could tell a native family from a foreigner not just by their clothing and appearance but also by their behaviour. The locals are more reticent or shy. They have a restraint about them that is visible not just in their stiff, slinking, or awkward manners but also in their austere, nearly shuttered looks. They'd eat silently, staring at the empty space like mute bazaar dolls. The foreigners, on the other hand, are jovial and chatty. Their behaviour is comfortable, their faces relaxed, and their eyes bright. Looking at them, one gets the impression that they are willing to converse casually with the first person who comes up to them. They are clearly not choked by the burden that crushes locals. Nothing, however, suggests that the war is approaching. For many of my fellow compatriots, the hotel's social life provides an escape from the daily routine.

As the evening grew dimmer and more electric bulbs were turned on, I could see the garden being invaded by waves of night and light pushing through the glass wall. The moon was rising over the buildings surrounding the hotel. It appeared to be gazing at me, like a featureless face still unfinished on a large painting. I saw a swimming pool in the garden's centre through the thick, entwined branches and the obscure leaves dancing in the chilling breeze. Around the pool, people sat on long chairs scattered beneath the trees, chatting or staring mutely at the dark water reflecting the moon-shine.

As the butler walked away, wishing me a lovely evening, I noticed that the European couple who had been with me in the lift had moved to the table to my left. The lady caught my eye and smiled; I returned her grin. She was a middle-aged woman; tall, slim, well turned and sculpted, with a round face, clear-eyed, golden-haired, thin-mouthed, and her curls wrapped around her shoulders, and she seemed to be having a good time with that man who appeared to be her husband. He was much older, stout, broad-shouldered, white-haired, with a greying small moustache, a high forehead, two prominent eyes, and a nose half a banana long and curved. He didn't grin but looked at me listlessly as if I were part of the furniture or didn't exist. They were both dressed elegantly for the evening. He wore a well-cut blue suit with a grey tie over a silky white shirt, and she wore a long dashing and streaming black gown that highlighted her feminine qualities in abundance.

However, I didn't notice the couple right away because I was preoccupied with Hassan and the Mughli being together at the time, and God only knew what they were planning. Even when I sat down with the menu card in my hands, gazing listlessly now at the card, now at the garden, it took a while for me to notice the presence of the two Europeans. And it was the lady's mysterious, keen, hinting perfume that had already dizzied me in the lift, that was fondling my nostrils and wheedling me again so rapturously that it was just impossible for me to remain insensitively unaware of her presence; such a perfume caused me to turn my head involuntarily after the first moment of distraction, to seek the source of that magical invasion whose charming sweetness I could hardly ignore. Then I noticed the couple, and when our gazes connected, the lady grinned, causing a true ravage in my bosom. And while I returned her smile, I couldn't help but wonder why such a polite fairy was dining with that ancient astronaut when I was alone and ready to entertain her. But I instantly repressed that crazy thought, just as I had suppressed the strange yearning to settle down in the restroom. Obviously, my mood is pretty quirky and even a little unsociable at the moment, which is most certainly a result of my sudden wealth.

It takes an entire world to become "nouveau riche." It is more complex than one might imagine. In fact, it may be confusing if one's wealth is a little imaginary, hypothetically speculative and excessively exaggerated.

I have a lot of money. The Director of National Security himself recognised it. Yet, I don't see it. A little voice whispers into my ear: "Who is the millionaire who sees his money, Bassam? Money is today just digital abstractions in mind." That might be true if it does not imply that the invisible is useless, does it?

You know what! This is tricky because being invisible does not mean being non-existent. We cannot see oxygen yet know it exists because we cannot survive without it. We cannot see the electromagnetic waves that transmit sounds and voices from an emitter to a receptor, yet what would our lives be like today if we did not have the telephone, the radio, the TV, etc.? Similarly, I recall being married once in the jail library, and while the witnesses are still living, my bride - alas! - has passed away. Allah have mercy on her soul! I don't see her, but she exists in the sky.

I am a widower, not a bachelor.

Take 'Ouja's imam and grand savant, Haj Mukhtar. He had married an invisible princess, and although she was from the Jin species, she had well introduced him to the fantastic realm of the unseen world. He has since socialised with Jin royals: princes, duchesses, barons, etc. When I inquired about him during my recent stay in the village, I was told that he had gained new powers because, following the death of his father-in-law, the Jinni King (which had nothing to do with the massacre; it had occurred some months before it), the princess was summoned to her dad's palace. She inherited her father's reign, and Haj Mukhtar became the King's consort of the jinni monarchy. This new status gave him a broader range of prerogatives. It kept him busy nearly all the time, although he had to be fair and make room in his agenda to the most urgent of 'Ouja's affairs. That included the Friday and the Eid prayers.

As King's consort and the father of the heir to the throne, he could no longer devote much time to the villagers and the patients who came from the farthest reaches of the country to seek his assistance and were thus frequently forced to wait a week and sometimes a month or two or more - I was told - until he returned from the invisible kingdom.

Everyone now knows that Haj Mukhtar has the ability to become invisible at will after the coronation of his wife as Queen of the Jin

Kingdom. But this is only one of his new powers. Some of 'Ouja's residents, whom I consider reliable, claimed to have seen Haj Mukhtar flying above the roofs of the town like a giant bird before fading into space. When I inquired, I was told that on the night of the Islamist Coup, one of the villagers was passing by Haj Mukhtar's house after he had spent the evening playing dominoes in the coffee shop. Suddenly, the sky flashed, and the dark night glittered with dazzling coloured lights and whistling and buzzing sounds. As the man lifted his head, he noticed a strange object flapping above the roofs, hovering just above Haj Mukhtar's house. It wasn't an aeroplane, a helicopter or anything known. The man came to a complete halt, and even if he had wanted to continue walking, it would have been impossible because he was screwed in the street like a nail lodged into the pavement. Aside from his eyes, which continued to see, and his ears, which continued to hear, he felt his entire body become as immobile as a rock on the mountain.

Meanwhile, he reported, the strange object, which resembled a large saucer, sprouted bright lights that blinked and sparkled in the darkness with all the iridescent hues of a hundred rainbows. The zipping and whistling continued for a time he could not assess before silence regained the evening. Then, finally, a door opened in the centre of the saucer, and a dazzling yellow light was projected on the roof. The witness swore by Allah and the Prophet that he saw Haj Mukhtar standing straight on the top of his house, dressed in white. At the same time, a ladder descended slowly from the saucer. He climbed its steps until he reached the door of the aeroplane that was not an aeroplane and was engulfed inside. The gate closed, the saucer whistled and whizzed again, the lights gleamed and blinked with all their brilliant colours, and the strange thing went whirling and swirling in the air, moving higher and higher at incredible speed until it swooned and vanished behind the mountains, becoming a star among the stars. And it wasn't until the saucer was high in the sky that the man who watched Haj Mukhtar's incredible trip could recover and reclaim his freedom. He estimated the duration to be unknowable because his wristwatch still indicated the time when he left the coffee shop. It was as if he did not walk that distance from the coffee shop to Haj Mukhtar's house.

Since then, some locals became convinced that the Jins, prodded by Haj Mukhtar, had undoubtedly participated in the Islamist coup against the former president.

***

FOUR

There was one sceptic among the people of 'Ouja who heard the account about Haj Mukthar's night flight in the saucer. Mr Houssine, Dalila's father, who had already heard the story several times, thought it prudent to remind me that the man who claimed to see Haj Mukhtar climbing into a flying saucer on the night of the coup is known as an inveterate hashish smoker. It's hardly impossible that he was so stoned that he couldn't tell a cock from a donkey!

– Why should the Jins use a machine to fly? Mr Houssine asked before adding wisely: Those who use planes and similar machines are the impotent men, who can neither cross an ocean in one second nor drink its water and turn it into a desert, which are the Jins' deeds, as you know.

I admitted that because they can fly like birds, live in the heart of the earth like worms and ants, build palaces and entire cities at the bottom of the seas, and perform other seemingly miraculous feats, a plane, a flying saucer, a ship, or a submarine are ostensibly useless to the Jins. Furthermore, those guys have no tracks at all. They can build cities and monuments, destroy others, live in peace, or drag huge, innumerable armies to clash in the most fantastic wars, making our Second World War look like a childish game without ever finding any visible evidence of it, even if it may happen right under our noses because we can't see or hear them if they don't want us to know. Those who are fortunate enough to learn about such events are few and far between, and Haj Mukhtar is one of them.

I won't deny that the thought of an army of Jins, led by Haj Mukhtar, taking part in the Islamist coup attracted me and seemed as appealing as it was incongruous. So why not? An alliance between the human species and the Jins might be immensely beneficial to both peoples. This is a reasonable assumption. Haj Mukhtar execrated the Scoundrel's reign and did not even try to hide his disdain. Naturally, equipped as he is by his vast knowledge of the occult and the paranormal sciences and strengthened by his kin association with the Jinn Kingdom, he fears nobody and could have changed Hamda La'war into a dog, a monkey, a donkey, or even a stone if he so desired.

Hamda did not approve of Haj Mukhtar's recent marriage to the Jin female because he was already married to Mrs Zubaida, Hamda's wife's sister. They were neither divorced nor separated. But he couldn't do anything about it other than mockingly repeating, "It's polygamy!" That happened when Haj Mukhtar told us about his marriage in the invisible realm. We were enjoying some new wine, offered to Hamda by a farmer, over a hearty dinner, as we used to do every Friday evening at the mayor's house. Haj Mukhtar questioned him, saying, "What's wrong with polygamy?"

– What's wrong? I'll tell you what's wrong. My wife and her sister are unhappy!

– That's it?

– Right. That's it!

Haj Mukhtar remained silent for a while. He downed another glass of wine and said:

– I am the Imam of 'Ouja, right?

– Yes, you are, said Hamda.

– When I told you wine and spirits are not sins in the Koran, did you believe me?

– You said no verse forbids alcoholic drinks as the Koran did for other acts, like eating pork, marrying his mother, sister, daughter, aunt, etc. So, yes, I read the Koran, and I believe you.

– How about polygamy, said Haj Mukhtar. Is it a sin?

Hamda remained silent, and the Imam went on:

– No, it is not. The prophet married several

females, and so did his valourous companions. Do you think we are better than them?

– I don't think anything, said Hamda, but my wife and her sister are unhappy.

After a while, Haj Mukhtar avoided our Friday meeting. He was reported sick and confessed privately that his Jin wife did not approve of our nocturn bacchanals in Hamda's house. Hamda continued to trash him, stating to anybody who would listen that the old man was a charlatan who takes advantage of the government's tolerance and the populace's stupidity. After a long friendship, the two men became the village's biggest enemies. Haj Mukhtar had been barred from leading the faithful in daily prayers and could only do so on Fridays. He pretended he was too busy with Jin State affairs, but Hamda told me he fired him.

It could have been simpler, but the mayor imposed another condition. Henceforth, Haj Mukhtar was not allowed to write his own Friday sermon. It would be prepared for him in the Party's cell and printed out. He would only read it to the faithful without changing even a comma. That was the drop that killed the frog!

The old man erupted in rage, swamping and trampling Hamda La'war, the Mufti, and even the President of the republic!

Haj Mukhtar couldn't tolerate reading a copy of a formal speech devised in the capital by the Mufti and given to all mosques for the Eid prayer. How could he accept a sermon drafted under the supervision of the one-eyed Party's cell?

That was a 'Bid'a' (i.e. anti-tradition invention) and hence could lead a faithful to eternal damnation rotting in hell. Previously, under the King, the Imams had always freely delivered their sermons. Binding people with a single speech was not only uncomfortable to the spirit of freedom that Islam brought to the world, but it was also a sin, although not mentioned in the Koran, like spirits. Furthermore, the old man was irritated by the panegyric nonsense he was forced to read each Friday because he was certain that the President had prostituted the country and sold it off to Western powers for a golden retirement in Europe or some paradisial land the day he would be ousted.

However, the Westerners were not waiting for the Scoundrel to take over to buy the country from him if they ever wanted to buy it after leaving it. Their civilisation has spread all across the world. Our children read their books while learning about our traditional culture. Many people prefer to further their studies in Europe or the United States. Their diplomas are convincing for getting the most outstanding jobs anywhere, but ours are only an option for HR. Even though traditional customs are still a part of our lives, new-to-us technical objects and cultural symbols attack us. Aside from going to the mosque and fasting during Ramadan, what remains Arab-Islamic in our lives? Cars, computers, aeroplanes, telephones, and many other contemporary gadgets are all worldwide products of the West, so there is no longer a West or an East. What is the dividing line? Who can make the distinction?

But my next-door neighbour, Mr Marmeduke, who I assume is an unrepentant radical leftist, has a different viewpoint. He once told me that colonisation had not stopped. But, to my surprise, he added:

– If the soldiers and the colonial ruler had gone home, the Western-trained locals became the leaders, and some have dual citizenship, one foot in this country for grabbing power and one foot in Europe in case things turn sour. However, holding European citizenship is no guarantee against deviations. Neo-Imperialism needs lackeys and relays to maintain its grasp on the peoples of the Third World. Where will they look for them if not among the local elite of newly independent countries?"

Thus, if I had understood correctly, 'the neo-imperialism,' to use Marmeduke's term, was busy developing and educating our country's power elite even before independence! Isn't that sneaky? These coups and counter-coups were most likely taught to them by their instructors in Europe and America!

– If you want my opinion, Marmeduke said, it's pointless to teach the Arabs anything because most of them are dim.

– Dim? I protested. But this is like racist biases.

– Come on, Bassam! You can't say that to me. I've dedicated my life to educating your children to love and respect one another, while I was teaching them history, geography, letters, and the beautiful arts. So I am in a good position to pass judgement on these matters. This strange phenomenon, though, has piqued my interest. Your compatriots are brilliant students as long as they live in the West. But as soon as they set foot in their fatherland and are given some political responsibility, they forget everything they learned at our universities about respect for Reason, Freedom and Human Rights and resort to the cudgel and the chain to communicate with their people. How can you explain that?

I didn't explain it and did not answer the question. But if this is a local behaviour, what does the West, neo-imperialist or not, has to do with it? Westerners don't want to buy anything else from us besides oil or natural gas, and there's nothing more to sell unless we sell our souls. But who would purchase them? We should identify another customer who is neither from the West nor the East but has been a citizen of the world from its inception; that customer is none other than the Devil, and he would likely take care of any sad soul better than anybody else.

***

These thoughts came to me as I ate, and I'm unsure what triggered them. Was it the sight of this restaurant's eclectic crowd? Was it the attractive lady's smile, her perfume, the fact that I am newly affluent, or anything else? But in reality, It's none of my business whether lackeys or counter-lackeys head the country. I've already admitted that my mind got blocked when it comes to politics and refuses to add anything to its already clogged database. It becomes like the black screen of a computer that crashes and won't allow you to log in. Nonetheless, I am to be honoured as a National Hero soon. In that case, the source of such a prestigious award lies in my stock-exchange speculations rather than in my political theories of the zero and none.

Indeed, had it not been for my millions, I would have likely mildewed in jail for twenty years, as the shrink assumed. Hassan would never have thought of me as a potential brother-in-law. Why should he? And he would not have allowed me to visit my village after the disaster that killed my mother and fiancee. I understand that these are the advantages of the new rich, and I am determined to keep them warm.

Everyone in this hotel knew who I was,

where I was from, and why I was there. The servants are very polite and helpful, and I had the distinction of receiving the manager at my table while dining. He's a tall, vaulted man with greying temples, a large wrinkled forehead, clear eyes, a hooked nose, a pursed mouth, and a strong chin. He is over fifty-five years old and is dressed in a well-tailored dark suit and a bow tie of the same colour. He arrived with the butler, who introduced him to me before skidding away almost stealthily. I had stopped eating out of respect for the newcomer, but he pleaded with me not to bother and to continue eating as if nothing had happened.

– I know you must be pretty busy right now, he said as I chewed laboriously on a piece of rough steak.

– Mmmmm... yep... mmm... that...

– But for nothing in the world would I pass up the chance to make a new friend, let alone when the new acquaintance is Mr Bassam Bourasin in person!

– Oooh! Ahem... Too much kind! I'm flattered.

– It is an honour, sir. I've been told you're dining alone, and I know such an event will not happen again. I'm sure you'll be busy with guests, customers, friends, and so on the following days.

– Ahemmmmm... Not improbable...

– As a result, I hastened to greet you personally.

– Thanks...

– Not at all, sir; I just wanted to ensure that everything was fine and that you're quite satisfied...

– Quite... thank you... satisfied.

– I can provide you with a suite, sir. We have superior rooms reserved for our most distinguished guests.

I had to cut him off before he became a pain in the ass. He was seriously irritating me.

– Sir, my bathroom is pretty satisfying. I don't want anything else. Thank you a lot.

In my hastiness to get rid of him, the word "bathroom" merely slipped out, albeit followed by an undisguised emotion. But the manager widened his eyes and asked:

– The restroom? Then, as if speaking to a child, he smiled and added: It's nothing, sir. Our suites have many excellent bathrooms, and you should - I propose, sir - look at them.

I shook my head firmly.

– Nope. I'm not changing my bathroom.

I don't know why I became obsessed with the bathroom. The manager looked at me with his mouth wide open. He was probably wondering if I was a guy or a toddler! I read in his eyes this muffled question: "Mr Bassam, how do you run your business being such a blockhead?"

The European lady seemed discreetly interested in my strange conversation with the manager. However, I'm not sure she could overhear us, not only because the restaurant was buzzing but also because the loudspeakers, well concealed in the ceilings and walls, were still distilling the undulating waves of a piano playing. I caught her look numerous times, and she seemed occasionally frustrated or bored because her friend continued to devour his food listlessly, without saying anything, as if the world had no constancy outside his dish, fork, and mouth. I almost thought she wasn't enjoying his company, which... is weird thinking that I quickly dismissed.

A group of uniformed officers dined together at the bottom of the restaurant. They were exuberant and boisterous. Though it was difficult to understand what they were saying in the general row, they talked loudly and laughed openly. I observed a little man in the middle of them who appeared to be their commander. He had a bald head and a swarthy face, and he seemed nearly splenetic because he didn't laugh at their jokes. The two turbaned fellows of the lift were also dining nearby and appeared to be engaged in discussing how the Arabs would reconquer Spain.

Mr Ali, the hotel manager, was not about

to give up so simply; at least, not without one more desperate attempt to save the honour. He paused briefly before returning to the offensive with a new idea.

– Forget about the suite, Mr Bassam. I have more suitable options for you. Please don't mind me speaking so openly.

I popped another piece of steak into my mouth.

– Go ahead, yum yum.

– Thank you very much, Sir. I wish your kind assistance for a charity.

– Yes, of course, I managed to say between two mouthfuls of spinach and another bite of meat. Why you don't dine, Mr Ali? Do you need to eat? Sit down, please.

That escaped me and expressed precisely the opposite of my thoughts. So I hoped only that Mr Ali would decline the invitation. Which he did. Telepathy sometimes works nicely.

– It would be an honour, Sir, but the doctor banned me from eating anything after 7 p.m. In fact, I thought you would be interested in the party we're throwing very soon; it's organised by the Medina Safeguard Association (ASM), of which I have the privilege of being the Chairman. (Pause to let me digest what he just said). You surely know that the old city, which is the nucleus of the capital, is almost collapsing, he added as I chewed imperturbably. The walls and roofs of renowned homes and ancient structures are deteriorating and on the verge of crumbling. We must pool our resources and raise significant funds from generous and benevolent philanthropists to conserve these treasured monuments from decrepitude and degradation. If not, many families may find themselves without a place to live, adding to the already large number of refugees and victims of war escaping from the south and nearby regions and flowing over the capital. Our city will never be able to find adequate accommodations for all of them promptly and to live. They will become violent and misbehave. That means more crime and delinquency, more plagues and infant mortality. In short, disaster. We cannot rely on the government to maintain and operate the critical arteries of this city since the government is embroiled in a war that does not appear to be ending anytime soon. They require funds to sustain their war effort, just as the city requires funds to function normally. That's why the ASM decided to throw a fund-raising party, to which we invited the most prominent figures in banking and business and capable architects. These gentlemen are scheduled to gather in this hotel tomorrow. I am delighted that you will honour our gathering with your attendance.

To get rid of him, I said:

– Well, give me time to prepare myself. It wasn't on my to-do list.

– I apologise, Sir. We should have invited you before, but... um ... We were told you were not expected to return to the office for at least one month. It had been two weeks.

The fibber! The creepy little liar! I'm sure he had no notion of any individual wearing my name and my face two weeks ago, let alone inviting me to his party! I wondered whether Hassan or one of his men spread the word that I'm a wealthy guy, which would explain why they're all crawling at my feet like lizards.

– Who told you that? I inquired.

– Nobody, Sir, he reddened and stammered. I'm referring to your office, specifically your secretary.

I had no idea who he was referring to. Even during the golden days of 'Ouja Bank,' I had no secretary. So, to keep the challenge going, I asked him:

– Was it a man or a lady?

I felt a sadist delight seeing him struggle with despair for a minute as he mused. Then, he finally jumps with both feet into the trap.

– Sir, it was a lady, if I remember well.

– Ha ha ha! I laughed. You lost! It was a guy.

His face deviated into an impressionist painting, with many colours sallying forth and disappearing alternatively. For a short period, I admired the excellent work Renoir had created over that unassuming face. Then, feigning astonishment, he asked:

– Really? I believe you, Sir. My secretary was mistaken when she told me a lady had answered her call. She had either forgotten or needed to pay more attention.

– I hope you don't mistake me for someone else.

– It's not feasible, Sir. Are you not Mr. Bassam Bourasin?

– I am, indeed.

– Well, I'd like to invite you to our party tomorrow in this hotel.

– I gladly welcome your invitation, Mr Ali. However, if I cannot release myself for any reason, I will give you a contribution. Is it okay to give a thousand dollars cheque?

– Thank you so much, Sir. A thousand thanks. Last year, we received individual donations, some between $50,000 and $1.5 million; the less significant amount was around $10.000 and $20,000. But we accept all contributions, even 5 dollars, Sir.

I had the impression that he gave me these numbers to show me how much of a miser I was, and his ploy succeeded because I was progressively growing ashamed of what I proposed. Then, while I was ruminating, he added:

– What are fifty or even five hundred thousand dollars for all those homeless individuals, Mr Bassam? It's hardly enough to buy them basic food essential for survival, don't you think so?

– Mmmm... You know better. My business is tight right now, but I would offer you $1. 500,000, Mr Ali, because my heart is weeping for the homeless and underprivileged. I know. They'd be just as useless to the refugees and lost as a modicum of 5 dollars. Nevertheless, whatever the amount my office decides, I'd withdraw my donation if you don't want it.

– Oh, please, sir, don't misinterpret what I mean. Your donation is welcome, even if it is only a single penny.

Then, in a gush of generosity, I told him:

– Don't make a fuss about it. I'll give you at least fifty, sixty, or eighty thousand dollars, Mr Ali. I wish only that everything will be all right for all those homeless people and that you take good care of them.

***

FIVE

The hotel manager thanked me and lavished praise before departing nearly on tiptoes. He reminded me that the party would begin at eight o'clock in the evening and that he would be glad to introduce me to the association's board. The European lady appeared intrigued by the scene; she had just finished eating and sipped her black coffee, whereas her partner had left the table and was going to the loo. She grinned again, rubbed her golden hair with her palm, grabbed a cigarette from her handbag, and leaned against the table's edge, begging for fire. I stood up, glad and pleased to serve her, and reached for her cigarette with my lighter.

– Thank you very much, sir, she said as the flame illuminated her face.

I assumed the entire restaurant was staring at us, possibly scolding me for my bad intentions. What a shame! To light a lady's cigarette in public! Furthermore, she is a European, and her husband was absent! Such misbehaviour! I challenged the entire community. I indeed had some secret plan with the lady, and I wasn't even aware of all that until I noticed the eyes following us. I instantly regretted my thoughtless gesture and, under pressure, was about to apologise to the lady. But she exclaimed, to my astonishment and relief, without paying the slightest attention to the public:

– Mr Ali is very kind. Unless I'm wrong, I believe he came to ask you to his party.

– You are correct. It was just as you predicted.

– Oh, she said, blushing. I am indiscreet!

– No, you are not, ma'am. I know you're one of his guests because he bowed, greeting you on his way out.

– Oh, we've hardly met; but I'll accompany Robert. We might locate some fine arts enthusiasts. Have you seen the exhibition?

– It has only been twenty-four hours since I arrived here. I've just seen the hocus-pocus they sell in the shops out there so far. I don't believe that's the exhibition you're referring to.

– No, you're correct. I'm talking about the painting exhibition. The gallery is on the third landing. Robert is overjoyed since it has been crowded with people of all kinds for the past few days. Some, mostly the young, are extremely sensitive and inquisitive, and they constantly inquire about any detail they notice on the canvasses. Some admitted to me that they knew nothing about abstract art, but they came to take a look anyway. Isn't it intriguing?

– Yes, I responded, looking around anxiously. The young are curious! They did not lose hope for a better world.

– Oh, I'm so chatty. I may have retained you, sir, while your dinner cooled. I apologise.

– No, ma'am, not at all, I objected. I've

already finished. I'm delighted to meet you. Please, allow me to introduce myself. I am Bassam Bourasin, a businessman and fan of the fine arts.

– Oh, really! Amazing! Waterbird, Janet Waterbird.

– Please, don't leave, Mr Bourasin. Robert is just returning, she urged as I bowed and started to go.

I looked in the same direction as her gaze. I saw the tall, broad-shouldered man moving across the room, shoving his lumpy tummy between the white-clothed tables.

– This is Mister Bourasin, Robert, a collector of beautiful masterpieces.

– Ah, great! He exclaimed.

Mr Waterbird didn't even bother shaking hands with me. He just said, "Hi, how are you?" He seemed bored with the entire world. He sat down and began sipping his coffee listlessly, almost oblivious that I was still standing at their table. I excused myself and left. The server stopped me on my way out the door and said:

– Your dessert, sir.

– Thank you. Next time.

The butler then arrived and asked:

– May I assist you? Is something wrong?

– Everything is fine. I'm just in a hurry.

– I see, sir. I propose a coffee or medicinal plant concoction.

– No, thank you, I don't take these things. They're good, I'm sure. But not for me now. Please give me the bill.

The man seemed perplexed by my withdrawal, although he had been staring at me since I started chatting with the lady, like everyone else in the restaurant. That damned cigarette!

The waiter had already dashed to the counter. He returned with a little tray in his hand, which he placed on a nearby table, and I noticed that he had also brought the bill and a pencil. I stooped and signed the small sheet of paper before exiting. The butler followed me to the door, simpering and repeating his best wishes. When I arrived at the lift, I noticed the lobby was nearly empty. The stores had closed, and most customers were either in their rooms or at the restaurant.

***

The night was quiet, and I slept as soundly as a camel in the desert. I awoke unusually late in the morning. I had forgotten to draw the curtains, so when the warm sunrays brushed my face, I opened my eyes and glanced at my wristwatch. It was already ten o'clock. I should not have slept all morning. Even if I am a millionaire, one cannot begin a new career by sleeping all morning! Furthermore, I had made the decision not to change my habits. In my situation, one must always be very busy, so busy that one cannot even afford more than a few hours of sleep; in reality, I am fairly busy, though I am not sure what. (These notes, for example, have become somewhat of a burden.

I keep writing, but I'm not sure why anymore!)

Yesterday's conversation with Mr Ali, the hotel manager, convinced me that I should hire a secretary to handle my agenda and organise my business. If my company becomes important in the capital, I need to consider opening a new office, most likely here at the Sheraton, although it is expensive. My living standard is rapidly developing and changing. The snoozy days of honeyed, tiny 'Ouja are now a distant memory. I'm doing well. I also need to change my car, despite my attachment to it. What is the point of remaining sentimental when one is prospering? "Zerga" does not deserve to be forsaken, but life is life. It's getting old and clogged with mechanical rheumatism. I can't afford a breakdown on the capital's streets, with thousands of cars, buses, and other vehicles behind and ahead of me. It would be such a hullabaloo and a shame! I'm already feeling ridiculous just comparing the old, rheumatic Zerga to those young, splendid vehicles I saw in the hotel parking lot. Zerga stands out as a crinkling peasant's cart or a mummy fit only for a mule. But am I a millionaire or not? What the hell is going on? I must replace the out-dated mechanical mule with a new, reliable vehicle. Let's see! What am I going to pick? A Jaguar will be fine; they are both strong and fast. I will not, however, get a Rolls Royce; they have become too vulgar, as all of the Third World tyrants have not only obtained their Royces but are also utilising their back seats to cut off their opponents' throats. I would choose a Ford whose look attracts me. Nevertheless, I am disturbed by the repulsive story of Mr Henry Ford, reported to be one of Hitler's backers. I realise this is old history, but even after all those years, I am still too sensitive to the tragedy of the Jews to buy from Ford. I want a Mercedes or a BMW, but governments use them, and people would think my car is public property. Furthermore, it will not distinguish me from any other public servant, although I am now an entrepreneur whose funds benefit the government. I'm not sure which car I'll buy. Yet, I need to find a buyer for Zerga. I'm not going to send it to the cars' cemetery. Not so fast! Not so early!

I called the room service and told them I wanted my breakfast delivered to my door. Then I contacted the front desk and asked them to place a 'For Sale' notice on the windscreen of my automobile. I assumed that with so many visitors, it would not go overlooked. If it is not enough, I will buy a newspaper advertisement.

I called the Ministry of the Interior and asked to speak to the Director of Security afterwards. After QA about my identity and the object of my demand, they told me he wasn't in his office. I was sorry! As I had missed him the day before, I didn't want to miss him again, which I did though.

Someone knocked on the door as soon as I hung up the phone. It was the room service delivering my breakfast tray. I tipped the man before he left. I didn't have much cash, and it was time to think more practically. I had to contact my bank's headquarters. Like many 'Ouja Bank customers who lost their money in the horrible rampage that destroyed the branch, reimbursement was due.

I had to fulfil my promise, though. I am a man who always honours his commitments. I took out my chequebook and wrote down the sum I decided to donate to the Medina Safeguard Association: Only Four Thousand Dollars. $ 4000. I removed the many zeros I had ambiguously hinted to, reducing the amount and Mr Ali's expectations to more reasonable proportions. It's not because Mr Ali ingratiated me that I would be hooked to his game and offer him $1.500.000. What would I gain in the deal? Is it the pleasure of being a great charity donator? That pleasure, I can live without it.

I inserted the cheque into one of the hotel envelopes I found in the room and put it in my pocket. I barely noticed that the cheque needed to be cashed only at 'Ouja Bank. Because the latter had vanished, I had nothing to fear but its reappearance, which would not occur tomorrow. In any case, even my previous account was not in foreign currency. I didn't have a single dollar in my 'Ouja Bank account.

I breakfasted, showered, shaved, put on my tweed jacket, white shirt, and blue tie, and was about to change my trousers when the phone rang, and I hurried to answer it. It was Hassan. I sat on the side of the bed in my underpants, the light sloping cheerfully through the balcony glass and bunching around my nude knees.

– Good morning, said Hassan. Have you slept well? I didn't want to bother you. I assumed you were tired after your journey.

– I appreciate it very much, sir. Everything is fine with me.

– All right, then get ready. I'll dispatch the car to pick you up... In fifteen minutes, say. The Minister will give you an audience.

– So fast? I was stunned.

– Yes, and please, don't keep him waiting. You should be here in five minutes.

– As soon as possible, Mr Hassan. But I must

tell you that I did not have the time to prepare the memo...

– It is not required. Following the meeting, you will prepare the paper. In any case, we have everything ready for you. Just drop over for a little chat. (He took a breath)... And in the name of Allah, I don't want to see you undone, so put on a tie.

***

SIX

The line clicked and buzzed. As I hung up the phone, I felt the sweat dripping down my temples and cheeks. I was surprised and impressed to get a meeting with the Minister so soon. I've never met a Minister in person, and I was well aware of the importance of the audience. Nonetheless, I was nervous. I'm done if I can't persuade the Minister that I'm the right man for the appropriate job. But which job were we going to negotiate about? I had absolutely no notion. I had no idea what to expect from myself. What if the Minister inquired about my recent activities? Should I state I'm a bank clerk or hint at my covert dealings? Perhaps that is the very subject to avoid. Absolutely!

The Minister should not be aware of my snooping for previous administrations. Hassan had pledged that the secret reports would be destroyed or kept out of their hands, and his sincerity was demonstrated by his eagerness to introduce me to the big boss. Then I had to prove my allegiance. I decided to tell him immediately about the strange news I had heard in 'Ouja. I'm almost certain the Afghan is devising a dreadful conspiracy against him. I know he set up a network of spies and dispersed them across the country under the fictitious cover of the Islamic Militia. He may be infiltrating the Ministry of the Interior at the moment. He must be stopped before he becomes too powerful to be driven.

I decided to bring the topic up with Hassan to address it with the Minister.

I removed the tweed jacket and replaced it with one more formal and appropriate for the audience. As usual, I emptied my pockets, drew out the contents, and placed them into my jacket pockets. Then, sprucely clothed, I lingered in front of the glass, smoked a cigarette, raked the remains of the cold coffee in the cup, and dawdled on the balcony, distractedly glancing at the white roofs languishing in the sun rays. The sky was deep and serene, with no cloud to mar its unruffled calm. I could feel myself getting stiff and sweating profusely under my clothes. I closed the glazed balcony door and pulled the curtains to enjoy the calm and cold freshness of the air-conditioned room once again. I needed to focus my attention before the meeting. I drank some iced fruit juice from the mini-fridge. Someone knocked on the door. It couldn't be the chauffeur yet. I opened. The housekeeper was the only one there, and she asked if she may clean the room and change the sheets. I let her in. The phone rang just then, and I rushed to answer it. The hotel receptionist apologised for disturbing me and reported that the Ministry had dispatched a chauffeur to wait for me in the lobby. I thanked him and told him I was on my way down.

***

It must have been a bright morning, for I met Mrs Waterbird again in the lift. She arrived before me, and she was by herself. That was what I'd call a close encounter of the third kind! Why? Because of what occurred, or rather, what did not occur.

– Morning, Mr Bourasin. How nice to meet you again! she exclaimed.

– Morning, Mrs. Waterbird. How are you doing?

– I'm fine, thank you. But you can call me Janet.

I loved her easygoing manners, although I think she was more sophisticated than she appeared. Her arms were very white in the short sleeves of her light long gown, and her long slim neck was adorned by a golden chain whose extremity was hidden in the deepness of her proud bosom at that mysterious line of junction. I could guess the shape and sweetness of her breasts under the tight brassiere. She generously offered them to my sight, straightening her head resolutely while speaking and her golden hair undulated over her shoulders. She was roughly my height, if not slightly taller, due to her high-heeled shoes.

– I will. I am just Bassam.

– Hello, Bassam, she said, smiling.

– I thought you were on the third floor.

– No, the gallery is on the third floor, not our room.

– I'll visit the exhibition as soon as possible, maybe even this afternoon if I can free myself.

– Thank you. It'll be our pleasure.

The lift stopped on the third floor, and she left.

A tiny, swarthy fellow in chauffeur attire awaited me by the reception desk in the lobby.

It was not the same man who had driven me to 'Ouja. I stopped to leave the little envelope addressed to the manager at the reception desk, then strolled towards the gate, following the driver to the black Mercedes waiting for us.

I tossed myself on the marrowy cushion and tried to relax as the car nosed through the capital's streets, thronged with many vehicles and a faceless crowd. I looked out the window at people crowding the pavement or hunching in front of the shops. The coffee shops were busy, and life appeared to continue as usual. Nothing has changed since the Islamist coup. Just more weapons appeared here and there. Armed men replaced police officers at street junctions, but residents looked now accustomed or maybe indifferent to their presence. Since the King's deposition, guns, tanks, and military displays have become a part of our daily lives. With the conflict in the south threatening to crawl over the rest of the country, it was customary to see those groups of men parading through the streets, some walking and some riding SUV cars, with their rifles, machine guns, and other weapons flashing in the sun. I raised my eyes as I heard the thunderous roar of an engine louder than all the vehicles on the roadway. It was a police helicopter flying at a low altitude, scanning the roofs and the streets. It hovered briefly above us before disappearing in a clap-clap droning of propellers.

Mrs Waterbird's ravishing perfume was still in my nostrils. It was enough to turn and daze all the heads surrounding her. I'm unsure why I had a flurry of strange thoughts in the lift with her. It was the first time in my life that a woman provoked such a flood of stunning hallucinations in my mind that I wished for the lift to be blocked by a sudden electric breakdown, trapping me along with her in that tiny space with no way for us to go up or down or get out! Really! It's insane! I'm becoming overly silly and maybe a touch lunatic. My sudden wealth has ostensibly harmed my mind rather than improved my situation. In the presence of a lady, a gentleman should not entertain such foolishly profligate fantasies. What if the idea materialised and I was suspended twenty metres above the ground, trapped in that cage with Mrs Waterbird? Would it make her happy? The devil knows how that weird thought infiltrated my mind! I am not

Bassam Bourasin, if that vile and lecherous left-side angel did not sow it in my head. I can hear him laughing while gripping his stomach. I wish you'd explode, son of a bitch! You're such a jerk! No kindness, no respect for anything or anybody, right? Get lost and rot in hell, damn the bastard father that begot you!

That woman had asked you for nothing, and while I was making a big deal out of our casual meeting, you betrayed me and sowed trouble in my senses! You are sick and horrible! I'm sure you aren't an angel but a pork!

I hope Mrs Waterbird did not suspect anything about what occurred to me. The more I think about it, the more I realise that the lift could have stopped in response to that unbelievable delusion. Don't they say reality is a manifestation of our thoughts?

– Holy shit!

What would I have done then? Would she have objected if I kissed her? Just a little kiss! On the cheek, as a brother!

– Would that have resolved the issue for you, jackass?

– I doubt it.

– She would have slapped you.

– Uch! This whole story is a weird idea! I refuse to believe I conceived it.

– I tell you what would have happened. If the lift had been blocked, you couldn't have approached the lady because she would have shouted in terror and said you attempted to persuade her to leave her husband and come with you.

– Wrong! I never thought about it. Anyway, I don't recognise myself in this salacious story. Mrs Waterbird never complained about boredom or asked that I console her in any manner.

– Yet, she's now connected to your lust.

Admit it.

– I'm not admitting anything. As long as you follow me like a shadow, I refuse to talk to you.

Did she guess my thoughts? I wonder. Because women are said to be incredibly intuitive. What a shame if she did! She'd probably tell her husband, "That guy in the lift, you know, Mr Bourasin, who appeared so shy and reserved in the restaurant... You won't believe it, but he suddenly became brash. Today, he kissed me right here on the lips. I did not guess his intentions. I'd slap him if I did. I'm pretty sure I'd slap him indeed." Her nippy, bored husband would then respond, "Ah, really! That's it?" Everything would end there. I don't see him coming over to punch me in the lobby. I'd hit him on the nose before he moved, even if he's much bigger than me, with muscles, fat, and bones. I don't mind if he's upset. In fact, I wish he was angry so he could say something other than, "Ah, really! That's it?" What more does he want? I am, in fact, a gross pig! I had no idea until I met Mrs Waterbird in the lift this morning, but now I know.

It's hardly comforting to imagine oneself as a pig just minutes before meeting with a minister of the Islamic State. This happened. It was unavoidable. The attraction was almost unbearable. It was her eyes, her flesh, her look, and all the unsaid — the indescribable magnetism and the tiny space filled with electric desire.

I felt like someone who had let a splendid opportunity pass through his fingers without catching it. I regret it now. Why didn't I stop the damned lift halfway, kiss the lady, and do whatever our hot hell of flesh demanded? I'm oversensitive and delusional, or just a coward? I felt guilty, guilty, and wretched because I could not do what I knew she was silently soliciting. My anxiety kept me from taking the step. So many social barriers had been planted in my head long before the thought of making love to a woman in a lift came to me. The idea of that failure irritated me and placed me in a depressed, ominous frame of mind. I cursed Mrs

Waterbird and her hopeless perfume. It was the day I had been looking forward to for years. I would miss it and fail miserably because of her awful fragrance, which had disrupted my senses and sent me on the run. If I hadn't been able to restrain myself, I would still be in the lift bouncing with the lady, and I would have had to say goodbye to my business and all my ambitions. This is at least the most comforting aspect of the situation. I did not do it, all right! And while I recognise that I was incapable, I am grateful that my timidity saved me time. I should not have lit her cigarette in the first place because, from inside, I burned up with its sight when she planted it at the corner of her lips. I'm damned if I'm not in love with Mrs Waterbird! I'm dying for her, and her white, naked arms, delicious lips, and glorious breasts are pursuing me like damnation to the Islamic State's Ministry of Interior.

***

I had to think it over again to get it out of my head. I was alone with Janet in that lift when... the blackout did not happen. The charge did not stop moving, and I did not take her into my arms. We did not kiss rapturously, and we did not make love. So, for God's sake, why am I feeling so dreadfully guilty?

In addition, I'm thinking of Hassan. If he has any suspicions — and I know he has spies in the hotel — he is perfectly capable of bringing me to court, where I will be sentenced even before I open my mouth because I betrayed him, did not show up at the audience with the Minister, and shagged a female tourist in the lift — but they would say "raped," of course. I'm qualified for 25 years in jail, adding to the former 25. A life sentence that is! Then goodbye to the marriage with Sophia, goodbye to the High Merit decoration, goodbye to the millions awaiting me quietly in the Treasury, and goodbye to the *Dolce Vita*! These bleak pictures loomed on the horizon like thunder in a summer sky, forcing me to make sense of the obdurate mess clogging my mind. If I wanted to appear as usual, sober, and sedulous as I was before meeting Mrs Waterbird and her cold-buttocked husband, I had to forget about her and erase her image from my mind.

Moreover, I was furious about falling in love with a married woman. I tried to catch a glimpse of myself in the rearview mirror, but the shadow I saw reflected on the smooth surface shimmering in the sunlight had nothing to do with me. I lit a cigarette quickly, almost shaking my fingers, to regain my confidence before the critical meeting. I dared another look in the same mirror. The deep creases that formed on my forehead and the dark-hued crescents under my eyes nearly scared me. My eyelids were pasty and puffy, my lips were not grinning, and I had accidentally wounded my cheek when shaving. What a hot morning! I didn't even notice it in the lift mirror because I was distracted by Mrs Waterbird's face, bosom, and the rest. The cut was clotted with blood. I took out my handkerchief and tried in vain to wipe it away. Then I wet the end of the cloth with my mouth and pressed it to the cut. I carefully rubbed it. That incredible moment had passed. Last night's long sleep did not improve my appearance.

***

SEVEN

The Mercedes came to a complete halt in the middle of the street. We were temporarily sucked up in the massive gridlock. The other vehicles were honking and making a lot of noise. On the right, I noticed people gathering around the theatre's white stairway. Some of them were waiting for a car or a bus or something, sweating in polo shirts and t-shirts under the scorching sun, flinging its blistering arrows from the inflamed zenith. Others, mostly young people, sat on the bare slabs, staring carelessly at the vehicles. They didn't seem to bother or care about anything, including heat, dust, or noise. What did they expect? What would one expect in such a location at such a time? There was nothing to anticipate or hope for. They just sat down there or stood near the grey wall, empty-headed, light-hearted, accustomed to their long-term jobless status, without anxiety, like pieces in the theatre decorum, acting figurants in the daily play of their city, similar to the trees, advertisement posters, and the coffee shop tables. Indifferent to the town that reciprocated their indifference.

Then I wondered: why shouldn't they be there? If they were absent, I'd feel something important was missing in the capital! The governments come and go, coups, counter-coups, revolutions, counter-revolutions, right, left; they are still there, watching the vehicles and breathing the street's dust. They are the lucky ones! They don't have to worry about the future. They decided a long time ago: there's no future! I remember seeing that sentence written in black on the city's white walls for many years.

Ahead, near the corner of the right sidewalk, some people gathered before a modest fast-food cart distributing its sandwiches on the street. I could nearly smell the spiced scents of barbecue, Shawarma, Kebab, and other types of meat being prepared on the embers of a crude gridiron by a bulky fellow in worn white clothes. The merchant was happily singing, enveloped by a cloud of grey and blue smoke.

Some Europeans, possibly journalists, were going down the street with cameras slung over their necks and shoulders, and a dusky boy holding a straw basket full of handcrafted items was sprinting after them and shouting something. He was probably trying to market his equipment. Fortunately, Europeans continue to visit the country. I don't think they are tourists, for it is unlikely that they will ever see the golden dunes of the south other than on postcards.

Many shopkeepers had hung a giant poster of the Emir in front of their window shops as a talisman to protect them from the 'bad eye,' and the zeal of the militia, secret police, and various government spooks. The former pubs and bars had felt the direction of the wind. They quickly shifted their business to the Islamist-friendly trade of coffee, tea, lemonade and soft drinks. Iced water would quench the thirst of European visitors and good Muslims. The prohibition law was the first measure enacted shortly after the coup, and anyone who violated it faced harsh punishment. The Islamist government has been creative. On TV, a zealous journalist declared that we did not invent prohibition in modern times. The USA has long preceded us, thus recognising the harm of alcoholic drinks being banned in Islam. And the studio audience acclaimed by shouting, "Allah Akbar!"

On the street, the commotion was deafening. There was not only the roar of the engines, the pip-pip of the klaxons, the ding-dong of bicycle bells, the whistling of trams, the shattered groan of pedestrians, but also the loud whizzing and buzzing of the radios, the shrill voices of the pedlars, and the songs of popular singers howling and wailing over their disastrous love stories. The chauffeur had not said a word since we left, so I asked him if the ministry was still far away.

– No, sir, he answered. The Ministry is only at the end of the block.

Then we slowly drove out again, and it appeared to me that if I had walked, I would have been at the Ministry before the automobile. That's what I told the driver when trying to converse with him. I knew where the Ministry was, although I had never set foot there; yet, he appeared tired or wary and responded laconically with a simple 'yes sir'. His muteness did not help me change the direction of my thoughts. The Mercedes then picked up the pace, sliding smoothly and almost silently on the macadam, skirting the slow queue of vehicles on our right before pulling out in front of a high grey building whose iron gate was guarded by several policemen mounted with machine guns. The chauffeur jumped out of the car and hurriedly opened the gate for me before I could move.

The armed men dressed in uniforms saluted me, and a man in civilian attire rushed to greet me on the threshold with a honeyed smile.

– Mister Director of National Security is waiting for you, sir. Please, this way.

I followed him to the lift, whose door was open. The lift operator heeled us and pressed a button. The door slammed shut, engulfing the three of us. I was nervous. I looked at the mirror, pretending to fix my tie. I tried to appear relaxed and confident and attempted to engage the officer in conversation.

– It's a hot day, I said.

– Yes, sir, it's hot outside.

– The sun is really crushing.

– Yes, sir. Crushing.

– Wouldn't we suffocate if we didn't have air conditioning?

– We would, sir.

– There isn't a single cloud in the sky, which is unfortunate.

– Yes, sir.

– It may become a disaster for the farmers.

– Sir, yes.

– But we don't need rain, for we have oil and gas income, enabling us to buy half the products of the world. Ha Ha Ha!

– Yes, sir, he said with a forced smile.

– We are fortunate that oil and natural gas are Allah's gifts. It is evidence that God loves us because we are good Muslims, right? Why did he not give hydrocarbons to the Europeans? He loves us more. We are the people selected for paradise, aren't we?

– Yes, sir. We are.

– Unfortunately, we can't drink oil, can we?

– No, sir.

– It's like drinking alcohol. It will kill us, right?

– Right, sir.

– That's why alcohol was forbidden. Allah knows better than us.

– Yes, sir.

– And he loves us.

– Yes, sir.

– Moreover, oil is now in the hands of the Scoundrel. May Allah curse him!

– Yes, sir. We arrived.

The lift came to a halt, and the gate opened. Bowing slightly, the officer insisted that I pass before him, which I did. My short monologue with that UGO (unidentified government officer) had put me at ease before the crucial meeting. Since hope and self-esteem had been restored and confirmed after the damages of 'The Ouja catastrophe, I felt ready to meet the Emir himself, not just his Minister. After all, I murmured under my breath, as a reminder, my money now supports the government. It's for a good cause, as we will restore the Golden Age of Islam. The State would be in trouble if I demanded immediate payback. Right now, the war effort requires every penny available in the country and abroad to be in the central bank. I could neither require a complete and regular payback for fifteen years of laborious and patriotic services nor force the government to give me my money. I have no tanks, guns, or intention to mount another coup or counter-coup and call it a revolution, counter-revolution, devolution, or couvolution. Enough of this shit! We need centuries to get over it. The only consolation is that I am walking inside the Ministry of Interior as a VIP.

I have long dreamed of meeting the highest authority, which would open my way for a national medal like Hamda La'war. But even my one-eyed former boss did not put foot here despite his bragging. His wife said he disappeared! Where? Did Haj Mukhtar take him on a journey in the invisible world of the Jins? Their relationship has been limping, though. I hope Hamda was not arrested. When I think of all the people who never reappeared after they entered this building, I feel a shudder running along my spine. I heard some stories in prison. It's not comforting to guess what a sad job they perform in the most ominous ministry, but I have no choice.

We made our way along a carpeted corridor with high bare walls. Some office doors were open or ajar, and their occupants stared listlessly at me as I heeled the small fellow in a poor grey suit and shabby tie half-strangling him, speeding towards a large padded gate at the end of the corridor.

As we approached, he came to a halt and respectfully tapped the door with his knuckles, then twisted the knob and barked, "Mister Bassam Bourasin is here, sir."

A big moustached face appeared in the doorframe, two dark eyes darted at me, and the head vanished. Soon after, a tall bearded man came out and greeted me pleasantly. We shook hands, and he led me into the antechamber, where he asked me to sit in the armchair and give him a minute to notify Mr. the Director of my presence. I thanked him and sat down, gazing at the room's luxurious furniture. The other office occupant, whose face had appeared and suddenly faded, mumbled some apologies shyly and left the room with the man who had accompanied me upward.

I didn't have to wait long. The secretary knocked on another cushioned door and unlocked it. "Your guest has arrived, sir," he said.

Then, from the other office, came Hassan's familiar voice: "Let him in, please."

The secretary turned his head. Then opening the door to allow me in, he invited me with a motion of his open hand. I stood up and crossed the distance to the office.

***

Hassan stood in the centre of the spacious room, which seemed sumptuously furnished with rich carpets, a mahogany desk and oblong tables, leather armchairs, soft sofas, satin curtains, transparent lustres, and many other handcrafted adornments that mixed the traditional style with the ultra-modern setting.

– Welcome to the Ministry of the Islamic State, Mr Bassam, said Hassan as we shook hands.

I thanked him, and as I looked at his elegant blue suit and the sumptuous surrounding, I could not help but remember his pitiful look a few times ago in prison. All Praise to God! I told myself. The change is like magic!

– I don't order a coffee for you, he continued, since we need to see His Excellence the Minister straight away. But please, have a seat. I need to call His Excellence first.

– Can I smoke?

– Yes indeed, but only here, not in His Excellence's office, he said quickly and walked over to his desk.

I drew a cigarette from my packet and lit it as he dialled a number on his desk phone.

– Hello, sir. Yes, your Excellence! He's here... thank you, Excellence.

He replaced the receiver and turned back to face me. His clear green eyes were lively, and he seemed to be cheerful. He was probably having a good time. They say power is an exhilarating narcotic with well-known euphoria, which is why giving it up to a rival is so terrible.

– His Excellence will meet us in five minutes. Please, be ready.

– I am, sir.

The air in the large room was cool and refreshing, yet I was still sweating. I took out my handkerchief and wiped my neck and brow. Hassan was also smoking quietly, although he appeared cooler than I was.

I stared silently at the mahogany desk with its gleaming black polished wood and the long-backed plush chair behind it, imagining myself sitting there as Director of National Security. Then I pondered what would happen if I stood up, walked to the desk, and sat on that chair.

– Funny! My dear Bassam, you make an excellent director!

– Really? Why don't you go home then? I'll stay here to do what should be done for centuries in this country.

As he looks surprised and shocked, I add:

– Who said I'm not the Security Director, Hassan? Please call the Minister and ask him if you don't trust me. Come on, pick up the phone.

– How much did you say they owe you? The director of security asked, breaking the silence and luring me out of my reverie.

We rapidly returned to the former situation, he at his desk, me in the armchair. Were they going to give me all that money? I couldn't believe it. In fact, despite my confidence that I have certain rights, I never thought they would pay me for anything. Nothing, however, required them to respond positively to my assertions, not only because the regime had changed but also because there was nothing to prove that I was on the payroll of any of the Ministry of the Interior's sections. There is no such bureau as the one where I was claiming money. Nobody doubts that our Ministry's first job was spying on citizens and residents using invisible and trackless ways, though.

Otherwise, I had no legal status on which to build a case and claim my rights. Then I remembered the descendants of the spoiled jews. It occurred to me that my speculations and claims were similar to those of the Jews with the Swiss banks. Like them, I had every piece of paperwork proving my rights, and I was expecting that the new regime would recognise them, which meant that they would finally see me as their adversary - because I was spying for their predecessors - and pay me for it... in real cash! I am the spoiled Jewish of the Islamic regimes that ruled my country. What a great and elating feeling!

So, how can I define Hassan? This is a guy I couldn't outline. Since his skin is so thick, light strikes it and immediately reflects back. He emits no light at all. Actually a black hole. Where's the truth? Hassan was either a jerk, a cynical, a hypocrite, or an unrestrainedly immoral mind devoid of principles, values, creeds, and faith... In a word: a scoundrel! Another scoundrel, still undiscovered, unlike the ousted president, they're fighting.

Right! I used the identical phrase that had earlier caused him to flash while speaking it mechanically:

– Patriotism is too flattering to forsake, even if it would cost me $200 million, sir.

– Right! But nobody is paid in dollars here unless you have a foreign contract, he said.

– Please convert them to local currency; I don't mind. The only purpose was to simplify the calculation.

After a little pause, he went on:

– Well, I checked, you know. I'm sorry to say that your name does not appear in the Treasury's registries.

I pretended to be surprised and said:

– Oh! How about the Central Bank?

– Same thing.

– What about the Interior Ministry?

– Ahah! Do you need me to tell you that you're standing right at the edge of a cliff right now? If you admit you worked for them, you are out of the game. The payment you receive will be in a very different currency. Do you want to cause trouble? You demanded that I obliterate your reports while simultaneously demanding payment for them! It doesn't make sense. Some consistency, Mr Bassam. Are they all fools?

He must have read my thoughts. I have escaped Hamda La'war to fall into the grip of this creep, maybe not much different and perhaps even more ruthless, for my skull is now in his hands. How could I endure a relationship that was so unbalanced? I had no control. He could send me back to jail right away. I may become one never heard about again after coming to the Interior Ministry. They are hundreds, I was told, maybe even thousands!

As I didn't respond, he said:

– Anyway, you'll get compensated.

My heart was about to explode. I tried to calm down while choosing my words carefully:

– Sir, I truly don't need that money. Well, in fact, I don't believe that the State owes me anything. I was joking, merely joking, I promise you. Subsequently, I am sure that I owe everything to the State, from my food to my home and clothes. Even my life, I owe it to the State, sir. That's why I intend to be as devoted to the State as you are yourself, for you are actually my model and guide, sir.

No man is insensitive to flattery. Vanity is our weakness. It expelled Adam and Eve from paradise, as all monotheistic religions say. Softened by the ingratiating cajolery, he laughed. The tension in the Director of Security's office then dissipates as if by enchantment.

– No problem! Now look, Bassam. You must agree to a contract and work hard to earn your $200 million.

Dumbfounded, I repeated:

– A $200 million contract?

– Right! The money represents your share of the helicopter deal you won for the Ministry.

I stuttered even more stunned:

– Sir, I... I...

I intended to say, " I don't remember such a deal." I need to find out what helicopters he was talking about. When did I win such a deal for the Ministry? In this life? I was in prison. In another life? Maybe! But I need to remember.

He cut me off as I was stuttering.

– Bassam, shut your trap. Now, let's be serious. Since you have such poor memory, please remember that you negotiated this agreement with a British airlift company on our behalf. Are you okay with this? Although we have already received some of the helicopters, the contract, signed by the previous administration, provides for the importation of those helicopters for a total price of $699,000,000 and still needs to be paid. Do you agree with me? Our government will pay the cost of the helicopters and uphold the obligations and debts of our forebears. You will thereby fulfil your end of the bargain. Is it obvious? We will pay you $200 million because you obtained a discounted price. This also is stipulated in an annexed contract to the main deal.

It was as if he had thrown me from the highest altitude those helicopters could reach into the sea! Granted, I have a parachute. Still, I need to know how to activate it. That was urgent for me to learn, as a matter of life or death. Noting my perplexity, he added:

– You don't need to say anything. I know. You're tight right now, so let me take care of the payment.

Another pause.

– Look, Bassam. Don't take it tragically. It's good news for you, isn't it? Nobody would give a damn about you apart from His Excellence, the Minister, and his Director of national security since no one truly knows who you are or what you were doing. You are a perfect anonymous. No family. No friends. Only us. We are your true friends. Nobody will believe your story if you talk about what you heard in this office. You'll be officially categorised as crazy and spend the rest of your life in a psychiatric hospital. In prison, you still have hope to obtain relaxation. Not in a psychiatric institution, you know this. Remember, Mr Bassam, that this is a new regime; as such, we have the absolute power to create and destroy anything. Absolute power means the ability to recreate you. You weren't anything, but now you might become somebody on the condition you behave yourself. Let me give you more clues to understand your present situation and where you are, where you could be, and who you are dealing with. We - His Excellence and me - knew about you, your secret reports, your relationship to Hamda La'war and Laroussi Mamitu, and your double identity since you were in 'Ouja, not since we met in jail, as you may assume. I'll tell you more. I wasn't jailed, actually. I was deep undercover for a special mission. It is now *mission accomplished*. That's why you're here. I set up this deal for you, for your best interest. Don't act foolish and pretend you don't understand that you're assigned a classified mission. You have no choice. You are a spook, and spook you'll remain. You worked for One-eyed Hamda. He did not pay you. Now, you work for me, and I will make you rich. Is it not much better? You'll do exactly what I tell you to do. Don't think. We devise any plan. You just execute it.

He stopped. I didn't say anything. I knew that it wasn't everything. He has more to say, still. Did he forget we just had five minutes before the minister's audience? It's really unbelievable. He lied. God knows when they arranged everything.

– You are a spy, and what you did was not as innocent or unnoticed as you seem to think. No one in the Islamist government has as much knowledge of our nation's governance as I do. The majority of them are new to politics. This is my revolution, my day and my hour. In my dreams as a subaltern intelligence officer, I thought about it day and night for years. I waited for the moment until it came. You were part of the network of informers and agents I had established over the years. You assisted me even if you were unaware of it. Even though I have been your supervisor for years, you could not have known. Because you thought that Hamda La'war was your boss. He was actually one of my agents. The government changed. But without the boost from the Intelligence Services, everything would have stayed the same.

(Pause).

– We succeeded. Both the coup and the counter-coup are ours. The revolution and the counter-revolution are ours. We created both. We assisted Abdelghani Abdelghaffar in removing the former president just as we have assisted the latter previously in removing the king. In short, we planned the counter-coup that ousted the Scoundrel when he got too dangerous and tried to fly alone. The fool believed he could rule without us. To eliminate us, he intended to create his own spy agency. He couldn't rely on us. He was so blind that he was oblivious that we made him. Now look, Bassam, I am not telling you all this because I like to brag; I wouldn't be at this post if I were a braggart. I want you to forget everything you did in the past and before coming here. You understand that you are only known to this government as the businessman who negotiated the purchase of those aircraft from the British company. If questioned, you will respond that you have offices in London and this city, specifically the Sheraton. Your relationships are primarily with businesses and financial organisations, and you weren't even in the country these last few years due to work trips.

" Bassam, you must now sign the documents," he said, pausing again to crush the last cigarette in the ashtray. "On that, everything is based."

Without waiting for my response, he quickly returned to his desk. While I watched in wonder as he quickly opened a drawer and took out a sizeable yellow package, he later returned and sat down next to me in another recliner. I was literally submerged in wet perspiring.

He calmly opened the large envelope, took out the " contract, " and handed it to me. He gave the impression of someone who had precisely calculated and mentally rehearsed all the elements of the game.

He sternly demanded, "Please review these papers and sign here."

I noticed a slight shaking in my hands when I picked up the sheets. Hassan then pulled out a little piece of paper and pushed it over the table so I could clearly see it.

– You are a lucky man, Mr Bassam, he said. Congratulations! You've struck it rich.

I quickly determined that the small piece of paper was indeed a cheque. Based on the lavish display of zeros, I deduced that I had finally been paid for work I had not performed at the service of the State.

It was a cheque for $200,000 in payment.

– It's merely an advance on the overall amount, he remarked.

More Coming...Stay Tuned.

***

ABOUT THE AUTHOR

- Writer /Journalist/ Senior Researcher: London

- *Published over 30 books and counting, (translations not included).*

- *Authored co-authored, edited, and published hundreds of daily/ weekly/ monthly briefings, reports and analyses, peer-reviewed articles, monographs, and books, about MENA region and international politics.*

- *Participated in many international conferences, either on the panel, as a member of the organizing team, or as a journalist.*

• Has been involved with the media since his early career, thus serving in different posts: reporter, investigation journalist, copy editor, cultural journalism, political journalism, editorialist, and Executive Editor.

• Translated several books/documents. Also reviewed translations for publishers.

•Member of several academic boards.

• Veteran columnist and commentator for the media.

*• Ranking in the top 10%of Authors by all-time downloads on **Social Science Research Network**.*

•You can follow him on this website:

https://hichemkaroui.net/

Email:

info@global-east-west.co.uk

www.ingramcontent.com/pod-product-compliance
Lightning Source LLC
Chambersburg PA
CBHW070404200726
48294CB00003B/1071